BE A GOOD FRIEND

Developing Friendship Skills

by Ben Hubbard

CAPSTONE PRESS
a capstone imprint

Capstone Captivate is published by Capstone Press, an imprint of Capstone.
1710 Roe Crest Drive
North Mankato, Minnesota 56003
www.capstonepub.com

Copyright © 2021 by Capstone. All rights reserved. No part of this publication may be reproduced in whole or in part, or stored in a retrieval system, or transmitted in any form or by any means, electronic, mechanical, photocopying, recording, or otherwise, without written permission of the publisher.

Library of Congress Cataloging-in-Publication Data is available on the Library of Congress website.
ISBN: 978-1-4966-9523-9 (library binding)
ISBN: 978-1-9771-5928-1 (eBook PDF)

Summary: Connections made with other people affect the way we grow and thrive. But it can be hard to make new friends and maintain old relationships. Learn how to connect with people, be a good friend, and get the most out of friendships.

Image Credits
iStockphoto: Courtney Hale, 6, 28, Prostock-studio, 26; Shutterstock: Anastasiia Kozubenko, 12 top, arrowsmith2, 29, Bestujeva_Sofya, design element, Brocreative, 20, 21, CREATISTA, 18, 19 bottom, Dmytro Zinkevych, cover, Jacek Chabraszewski, 22, Lemonade Serenade, 19 top, LightField Studios, 7 top, 8 bottom, Lisa F. Young, 9, mangpor2004, cover background, Microstocker.Pro, 24, Monkey Business Images, 4, 5, 14, 15 top, 15 bottom, 16, 17, 27 top, 27 bottom, Plasteed, design element, Prostock-studio, 13, seekeaw rimthong, 12 bottom, Sudowoodo, design element, 7 bottom, Tom Wang, 10, wavebreakmedia, 25, Yayayoyo, 8 top, yogi agus pratama, 11

Editorial Credits
Editors: Mari Bolte and Alison Deering; Designers: Juliette Peters and Sarah Bennett; Media Researchers: Jo Miller and Tracy Cummins; Production Specialist: Laura Manthe

All internet sites appearing in back matter were available and accurate when this book was sent to press.

Table of Contents

Introduction
Relationships for Life 4

Chapter 1
Making Friends 6

Chapter 2
Planting New Friendships 12

Chapter 3
Maintaining Relationships 18

Chapter 4
Toxic Relationships 24

Chapter 5
Lasting Friendships 28

    Glossary 30
    Read More 31
    Internet Sites 31
    Index 32

Words in **bold** are in the glossary.

Introduction
Relationships for Life

What does the word *relationship* mean to you? Simply put, a relationship is a connection between two people. In our lives, we have different relationships with different people. Our first relationships are with our families. As we grow older, we form new relationships with other people around us: relatives, teachers, coaches, neighbors, and friends.

Friends are some of our closest relationships. We make our first friends when we are children. Some of these friendships last only for a short time, while others can continue for our whole lives.

How Many Friends Should We Have?

Some people have lots of friends and other people have only a few. Sometimes, people go through a period of having no friends at all. The quality of a friendship is what counts. Good friends care for each other, enjoy spending time together, and respect each other. Having a good friend is a great feeling. It gives you confidence and makes you feel valued.

Chapter 1
Making Friends

Many times, we make our first friends at day care or play groups. Sometimes, these friends are friends for life. The older we get, the more potential friends we meet. New schools, classes, and activities bring people together who may not have had a chance to meet otherwise. But how do you actually *make* friends?

Saying "Hi"

Friendships often begin with a "hi" and a friendly smile. Doing this shows you are happy to see someone and sends them a signal that you are approachable. Being an easy person to approach is an important part of making new friends. Ignoring people or looking away when they greet you sends out a signal that you may not like them or are not interested in being friends.

Overcoming Shyness

Introducing yourself to new people can be hard. This is especially true if you are a **shy** person. But even people who seem very confident can be shy from time to time. The reasons for being shy are the same for everyone. We wonder: *Will the new person like me? Will they be interested in talking to me? Will they even acknowledge that I'm there?* It's natural to feel this way. But introducing yourself to new people gets easier the more you do it. It is a great skill to learn.

Don't Fear Rejection

Most people are friendly and polite when they meet someone new. But if someone seems rude or disinterested when you meet them, don't take it personally. Often, this means they are nervous or insecure. Give them a few chances to open up.

After Hello

Smiling, saying "hello," and having the confidence to speak to new people are all great first steps in making friends. But what then? How do you take the next step to become friends? And how do you know that your friendship will work?

Common Ground

Friends don't have to be alike, but finding common ground can help jump-start a new friendship. This can mean you like the same things, such as movies, music, or clothes. Or perhaps you have similar opinions about a sports team or class at school. Sometimes the common ground is that you both find each other fun to be around.

Be Nice

Showing someone you like them can take lots of forms. You might ask them questions about themselves, or give them honest compliments about the way they look or act. Small acts of kindness, such as sharing a snack or helping someone with their homework, are all friendly actions.

Chapter 2
Planting New Friendships

Starting a new friendship is a lot like planting a seed. You're not sure what will grow, but it needs to be nurtured and taken care of. This means taking things slow. You may think you've just met your new best friend forever (BFF), but you still need to respect each other's space and let your friendship grow naturally.

Providing Space

Good friendships are balanced. Both people should want to see each other equally as much. But some friends can behave **possessively**. They may want to take up all of your time or prevent you from being friends with anyone else.

You may even find yourself being the possessive one. Are you always suggesting things to do? Does your friend seem tired or irritated by that? If so, it might be time to step back and let them come to you next time. That way the friendship can grow naturally, without pressure being added.

Hanging Out

Having a new friend over is a great way of getting to know them better. This is all about fun, but also being a good host or guest when it's your turn. Here are some tips to help things run smoothly.

Being a Good Host

✓ Have some snacks ready.

✓ Prepare some games or activities in advance.

✓ Always let your guest decide what you'll do and let them go first.

✓ Make your guest comfortable at all times and be attentive to their needs.

Being a Good Guest

✓ Be polite at all times, especially to your host's family.

✓ Go with the flow to make sure things run smoothly for everyone.

✓ Share activities like gaming equally, so you both have fun.

✓ Read the room. If your host is hinting it's time to go, say your goodbyes. Be sure to thank them for the invite.

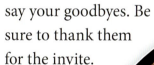

Connecting not Impressing

Good friendships are about connecting with people, not impressing them. But some people think they have to impress others to become their friends. They might **brag** about what they have done, show off things they own, or try to win you over by buying you things. These people appear popular and always seem to have people around them. But are they real friends or just shallow friends?

A Real Friend?

☹ Is the friend only glad to see you when they want something?

☹ Does the friend make unkind jokes about you in public to get laughs?

☹ Is the friend rude about other people behind their backs?

☹ Does the friend pressure you into spending time with them?

If you answered "yes" to these questions, your friend is not being a good friend. It might be time to find someone else to spend time with. ☺

Chapter 3

Maintaining Relationships

Every relationship has its ups and downs. Arguments and disagreements happen even with the people we like best. However, there are constructive ways of dealing with relationship **conflicts**. Here are some tips to help you through them.

Don't Yell

You may be furious with your friend, but yelling won't help. Instead, take some time and space to calm down. Come back to the friend when you are ready to make up.

Explain and Ask

After an argument, explain your side and your behavior. Be honest about your feelings. Ask about your friend's point of view. Understanding each other goes a long way to **resolving** a conflict.

Agree to Disagree

Friends don't always agree and that's OK. If you disagree over something that isn't physically or mentally harming someone, agree to disagree, and try to move on.

Talk About It

Even after the fight is over, there may be some conflict that sticks around. You may feel like you were badly treated during your fight. Or maybe there's an issue that's still unresolved. Talking these things out is the best way of maintaining a healthy relationship.

How to Talk Things Out

When you are discussing what happened with your friend, you will need to explain why something they did made you feel bad. Softening what you say can help prevent people from feeling attacked. Once you have explained both sides, you can think of a solution to avoid the same conflict in the future.

Instead of	Try
"I can't believe you..."	"I know you were just trying to..."
"You really..."	"I'm sure you didn't mean to..."
"Can't you..."	"I know it's hard for you to..."
"You should..."	"Next time, could we..."
"I think you should..."	"Going forward, let's agree to..."

Being True to Yourself

Pleasing a friend feels nice. Letting a friend have the first turn at a game or doing something they suggested are ways to make them happy. But over time, we may feel like we are doing this too often with nothing in return. Or perhaps a friend may ask us to do something we don't feel comfortable with. When this happens, we need to be true to ourselves and say "no."

How to Say No

Saying "no" doesn't have to be **hostile**, but it does need to be firm. Here are a few suggestions to help get your point across.

"No thanks, I'm not comfortable doing that."

"That's not the kind of thing I'm into."

"I don't feel like doing that."

"I don't want to do that. Could we do something else?"

"Thanks, but I'm happy the way things are."

Chapter 4
Toxic Relationships

What is the difference between teasing and **bullying**? A person may tease by laughing at the way you do something. This can be annoying, but it can also be just jokes between friends. Bullying, on the other hand, is a deliberate act of meanness that is repeated. Bullying is against the law and must be taken seriously.

Types of Bullying

There are many forms of bullying. A person or group may physically hurt you or take your things. They may call you names or **intimidate** you. Bullies can send nasty messages. They may encourage others to bully you too.

Tackle Bullying

If you are being bullied, you need to tell an adult you trust. Otherwise, the bullies will keep getting away with it. An adult can help you decide whether to involve your school or even the police if needed. It's also helpful to talk to your friends. They are on your side and it will help you feel less alone. Bullies want to cut you off from people who support you. Don't let that happen!

Walk Away!

Some relationships aren't healthy. They may be physically or mentally draining or damaging. Other times, you may have differences you just can't resolve. Unhealthy **toxic** relationships can put stress on both our bodies and our minds. Sometimes it's best to just walk away.

Healthy vs. Unhealthy Friends

Every friendship is different. You may meet your BFF when you're 5 years old. Or you may not have a best friend until you are a teenager or an adult. Some people make friends for life. Others make friends easily in new situations.

Most friendships are great but sometimes we attract the wrong type of friend. They may be a bully or user or someone who does not have your best interests at heart. These friends are unhealthy for us and we should seek better friends elsewhere. How do we tell unhealthy friendships from healthy ones?

An Unhealthy Friendship
Your Friend:

✓ is selfish and critical

✓ encourages you to do bad things

✓ isn't there when things get tough

✓ isn't interested in how you feel

A Healthy Friendship
Your Friend:

✓ shares with you and is there to help when you need it

✓ listens to you and cares about what you say

✓ comforts you when you're upset

✓ is gentle and kind to you

Chapter 5
Lasting Friendships

Empathy and understanding are important factors in retaining long-term relationships. Saying sorry, moving past conflict, accepting your friends, and showing them they are important are all ways of creating lasting friendships. They are also skills you can take with you into every new relationship.

Accepting Friends

Everyone has some annoying traits. Your friend might have an irritating eating habit or be supercompetitive with you. But this doesn't mean they are any less of a friend. Accepting your friends for who they are will help ensure the friendship lasts.

The Power of Forgiveness

We all make mistakes and say or do dumb things that upset the people we are close to. This doesn't mean we don't care about them. When a friend does something like this to you, you can tell them you are upset. But then the best thing you can do is forgive them. That's how good friends behave.

Glossary

brag (BRAYG)—to talk about how good you are at something

bully (BUHL-ee)—to frighten or threaten someone

conflict (KON-flict)—a disagreement

empathy (EM-puh-thee)—imagining how others feel

hostile (HOSS-tuhl)—unfriendly or angry

intimidate (in-TIM-uh-date)—to threaten in order to force certain behavior

possessive (puh-SEZ-uhv)—showing ownership or belonging

resolve (ri-ZOLVE)—to decide you will try hard to do something

shy (SHY)—being reserved or timid when around other people

toxic (TOK-sik)—something unpleasant or harmful

Read More

Bullis, Amber. *Empathy*. Minneapolis: Jump!, Inc., 2021.

Criswell, Patti Kelley. *A Smart Girl's Guide to Knowing What to Say: Finding the Words to Fit Any Situation*. Middleton, WI: American Girl, 2018.

Kenney, Karen Latchana. *Getting Out and Getting Along: The Shy Guide to Making Friends and Building Relationships*. North Mankato, MN: Compass Point Books, 2019.

Internet Sites

Parents: Relationships
parents.com/parenting/relationships/

Plant Love Grow: Friendship Building
plantlovegrow.com/friendship-building.html

Scholastic Parents: Friendship Lessons for All Ages & Stages
scholastic.com/parents/family-life/social-emotional-learning/development-milestones/lets-be-friends.html

Index

acts of kindness, 11
asking for help, 25

bullying, 24–25, 26

common interests, 10, 14–15
communication, 20
compliments, 11
conflicts, 18–21, 28
connections, 16

feelings
    anger, 19
    empathy, 28
    hostility, 23
    irritation, 13
    possessiveness, 13
    rejection, 8
    shyness, 8
forgiveness, 29

hanging out, 14–15
hosting, 14

lasting friendships, 28–29

maintaining friendships, 12–13, 18–20
making friends, 6–7, 10

pressure, 13, 17

relationships, 4–5
resolving conflicts, 19

saying no, 22–23

toxic relationships, 24–25

unhealthy friendships, 26–27